THE STUPID TIGER
and other tales

THE
STUPID TIGER
AND OTHER TALES
Upendrakishore Raychaudhuri

TRANSLATED FROM THE BENGALI
BY WILLIAM RADICE

ILLUSTRATED BY WILLIAM RUSHTON

ANDRE DEUTSCH

First published 1981 by
André Deutsch Limited
105 Great Russell Street London WC1

Copyright © 1981 by William Radice
Illustrations © 1981 by William Rushton

Printed in Great Britain by
Ebenezer Baylis & Son Ltd.,
The Trinity Press, Worcester, and London.

British Library Cataloguing in Publication Data
Raychaudhuri, Upendrakishore
   The stupid tiger, and other tales.
   1. Tales, Bengali
   2. Animals, Legends and stories of – Bengal
  I. Title
   398.2'45'095414   GR302.2.B44

ISBN 0–233–97256–0

Library of Congress Number 80 2691

Contents

THE STUPID TIGER
and other tales

1 The Story of the Tailor-bird and the Cat

IN THE YARD of a house there was a brinjal-plant. A tailor-bird had sewn up the leaves of the plant with her beak, to make a nest.

Inside the nest there were three tiny chicks. They were so tiny that they couldn't fly or open their eyes. They could only open their mouths and cheep.

The householder had a very wicked cat. She kept thinking, 'I'd like to eat that tailor-bird's chicks.' One day she came to the base of the brinjal-plant and said, 'Hello, little bird, what are you doing?'

The tailor-bird bowed her head till it touched the branch beneath the nest, and said, 'Humble greetings, Your Majesty.'

1

This made the cat very pleased and she went away.

She came like this every day, and every day the tailor-bird bowed down before her and called her Your Majesty; and the cat went away happily.

The tailor-bird's chicks grew big, and they grew beautiful wings. Their eyes were open now, so the tailor-bird said to them, 'Children, do you think you can fly?'

'Yes, mother we do,' said the chicks.

'Well,' said the tailor-bird, 'let's see first whether you can go and perch on a branch of that palm tree.'

The chicks flew off at once and perched on a branch of the palm tree. Then the tailor-bird laughed and said, 'Now let's see what happens when the wicked cat comes.'

In a little while the cat came and said, 'Hello, little bird, what are you doing?'

This time the tailor-bird kicked her leg at her and said, 'Go away, you good-for-nothing cat!' Then she darted into the air and flew away.

Baring her teeth, the cat jumped up into the plant; but she couldn't catch the wicked tailor-bird, or eat the chicks. She just scratched herself badly on the thorns of the brinjal, and went home feeling very silly.

2 The Story of the Tailor-bird and the Barber

A TAILOR-BIRD went to perch and dance on the leaves of a brinjal-plant. While he was dancing, he scratched himself on the thorns of the plant. The scratch grew into a huge boil.

Oh dear, what was to be done? How could such a big boil be cured?

The tailor-bird asked first one person then another. Everyone said, 'The barber will lance it for you and get rid of it.'

So the tailor-bird went to the barber and said, 'Barber, barber, please will you lance my boil?'

When the barber heard this he turned away his face, screwed up his nose and said, 'Ugh! I shave the king; how dare you ask me to lance your boil?'

'All right,' said the tailor-bird, 'we'll see whether you lance my boil or not!'

Then he went and appealed to the king: 'Your Majesty, why won't your barber lance my boil? He must be punished.'

The king laughed ho-ho-ho when he heard this; he lolled back on his cushions, and said nothing at all to the barber. This made the tailor-bird very angry. He went to the mouse and said, 'Mouse, mouse, are you at home?'

'Who is it?' answered the mouse. 'Tailor-bird? Come in and sit down, my friend! Have some rice—have something to eat.'

'I'll eat with you,' said the tailor-bird, if you'll do something for me.'

'What?' asked the mouse.

'You must go to the king when he is asleep and gnaw a hole

3

in his belly,' said the tailor-bird.

When he heard this the mouse bit his tongue, put his paws over his ears and said, 'What an idea! I can't do that.' So the tailor-bird went off angrily to the cat and said, 'Cat, cat, are you at home?'

'Who is it?' answered the cat. 'Tailor-bird? Come in and sit down, my friend! Have some rice — have something to eat.'

'I'll eat with you,' said the tailor-bird, 'if you'll kill the mouse for me.'

But the cat said, 'I can't go and kill mice now; I feel too sleepy.' So the tailor-bird went off even more angrily to the stick and said, 'Stick, stick, are you at home?'

'Who is it?' answered the stick. 'Tailor-bird? Come in and sit down, my friend! Have some rice — have something to eat.'

'I'll eat with you,' said the tailor-bird, 'if you'll flog the cat for me.'

4

But the stick said, 'What has the cat done to me to make me want to flog him? I can't do it.' So the tailor-bird went to the fire and said, 'Fire, fire, are you at home?'

'Who is it?' answered the fire. 'Tailor-bird? Come in and sit down, my friend! Have some rice — have something to eat.'

'I'll eat with you,' said the tailor-bird, 'if you'll burn the stick for me.'

But the fire said, 'I've burnt ever so many things today; I can't burn anything more.' The tailor-bird was angrier than ever. He went to the sea and said, 'Sea, sea, are you at home?'

'Who is it?' answered the sea. 'Tailor-bird? Come in and sit down, my friend! Have some rice — have something to eat.'

'I'll eat with you,' said the tailor-bird, 'if you'll put out the fire for me.'

But the sea said, 'I can't do that.' So the tailor-bird went to the elephant and said, 'Elephant, elephant, are you at home?'

'Who is it?' answered the elephant. 'Tailor-bird? Come in and sit down, my friend! Have some rice — have something to eat.'

'I'll eat with you,' said the tailor-bird, 'if you'll drink up all the sea's water for me.'

But the elephant said, 'I can't drink so much water; my stomach would burst.'

In the end, when he saw that no one else would listen to him, the tailor-bird went to the mosquito. The mosquito saw him coming and said, 'Who is it? Tailor-bird? Come in and sit down, my friend! Have some rice — have something to eat.'

'I'll eat with you,' said the tailor-bird, 'if you'll bite the elephant for me.'

'Nothing easier!' said the mosquito. 'I'll go at once. We'll soon see how tough that brute the elephant's skin is.' He called all the mosquitoes together from all around and said, 'Come on, my friends; let's see how tough that brute the elephant's skin is.' So all the mosquitoes from miles around, young and old, friends and relations, joined together and with a zing-zing-zing-zing flew off to bite the elephant. The

5

whole sky was covered with mosquitoes; they even covered the sun. A storm began to blow with the beating of their wings. Everyone trembled in alarm at the terrifying zing-zing-zing-zing. Then —

The elephant said, 'I'll drink up the sea!'
The sea said, 'I'll put out the fire!'
The fire said, 'I'll burn the stick!'
The stick said, 'I'll flog the cat!'
The cat said, 'I'll kill the mouse!'
The mouse said, 'I'll gnaw at the king's belly!'
And the king said, 'I'll cut that stupid barber's head off!'

The barber trembled and clasped his hands together and said, 'Spare me, tailor-bird, spare me! Come sir — come and let me lance your boil.'

So the tailor-bird's boil got better, and he was very happy. Once again he danced and sang — Toon-toona-toon-toon, drub-drub.

3 The Story of the Tailor-bird and the King

A TAILOR-BIRD had his nest in a corner of the king's garden. One day the money from the king's treasure chest was put out to dry in the sun; but when evening came his men forgot to take one of the coins inside.

When the tailor-bird saw this shining coin he picked it up and brought it to his nest, and thought, 'Ha! How rich I've become! I have the same gold in my house as the king has in his house.' From then on, he thought and sang nothing but —

> *The same gold in my house*
> *As the king has in his house.*

When the king heard this as he sat in his council-chamber, he asked, 'What's that? What on earth is the bird saying?'

'Your Majesty,' replied the courtiers respectfully, 'the bird is saying that he has the same gold in his house as you have in yours.' At this the king chuckled and said, 'Then go and see what there is in his nest.'

When they had looked they returned and said, 'Your Majesty, there is a single coin in the nest.'

'That must be my coin,' said the king. 'Go and get it.'

At once the courtiers went and brought back the coin from the tailor-bird's nest. What could the poor bird do now? He began to sing sadly —

> *The king gives nothing away:*
> *He has taken my gold away.*

When he heard this the king laughed again and said, 'What a cheeky little bird! Go and give him back his money.'

The tailor-bird was overjoyed to get his money back. Now he sang —

The king was very afraid of me:
He gave my money back to me.

'Now what is he saying?' asked the king.

The courtiers said, 'He is saying that the king was so frightened of him that he gave back the money.'

Now the king burst out in anger. 'So!' he shouted, 'that's what he thinks. Go and catch the rascal, and let me fry and eat him.'

The courtiers immediately went and caught the poor tailor-bird. The king held him in his fist and took him inside to his queens saying, 'You must fry this bird and give him to me to eat today.'

When the king had gone, the seven queens gathered round and looked at the tailor-bird.

'What a beautiful bird!' one of them said. 'Give him to me so that I can look at him.' So she took the tailor-bird into her hands. Then another queen wanted to have a look, and another. When the fourth queen was taking the tailor-bird, he slipped out of her hands and flew away.

What a to-do! What could be done now? If the king found out, there'd be no escape.

While they were weeping and wailing, a frog happened to plop past them. When the seventh queen saw it she pounced on it and caught it, saying, 'Ssh! No one will know. If you fry this and give it to the king to eat, he will think he is eating the tailor-bird.'

So they skinned the frog and fried it for the king; and when he had eaten it, he was very happy.

A little later he was sitting in his council-chamber, thinking, 'Now that beastly little bird won't bother me any more' — when the tailor-bird suddenly sang —

> *Funny dinner, funny dinner:*
> *The king has eaten frog for dinner.*

The king jumped up when he heard this. He spat, choked, spluttered, rinsed his mouth and did goodness knows what else. Then he roared out, 'Cut the seven queens' noses off.'

At once the court executioner went and cut the seven queens' noses off.

When the tailor-bird saw this he sang —

> *For letting one little bird fly off*
> *Seven queens have had their noses cut off.*

Then the king said, 'Go and catch the rascal! This time I shall swallow him. We'll see if he gets away this time.'

So the tailor-bird was caught and brought back to the palace.

'Bring me some water.' said the king.

The water came. The king filled his mouth with water, took the tailor-bird, stuffed him into his mouth, shut his eyes, and swallowed him in one gulp.

Everyone said, 'Now the bird has had it.'

But just then the king lurched and let out an enormous belch.

The courtiers stood up in alarm, and the tailor-bird came out with the belch and flew away.

'He's gone, he's gone!' roared the king. 'Catch him, catch him!' At once two hundred people rushed off and caught the poor tailor-bird again.

Then they brought some more water, and a soldier with a sword came and stood near the king, to cut the tailor-bird in two if he got out again.

This time as soon as the king had swallowed the tailor-bird he sat with two hands pressed over his mouth, so that he could not get out this time. The poor bird started to kick up a

terrible rumpus inside the king's stomach.

In a little while, the king screwed up his nose and said, 'Ugh!' — and suddenly everything in his stomach, including the tailor-bird, came pouring out.

Everyone shouted, 'Soldier, soldier! Strike, strike! The bird's escaped!'

In a panic, the soldier lunged at the tailor-bird with his sword. But he didn't touch him; instead his sword fell on the king's nose.

The king let out a terrible yell, and everyone in the council-chamber began to yell with him. Then the doctor came with ointment and bandages, and just managed to save the king's life.

Meanwhile the tailor-bird sang —

10

> *The king has lost his nose — Oh!*
> *See what I've done to him now — Oh!*

Then he flew off and left the country; so that when the courtiers came rushing to the nest, they found it was empty.

4 Narahari Das

ACROSS THE FIELDS and beyond the forest, at the foot of the high mountains, there was a cave; and in this cave there lived a little goat. He was not yet full-grown, so he couldn't go out of the cave. Whenever he asked to go outside, his mother would say, 'No you don't! The bear will catch you, the tiger will take you away, the lion will eat you up.' This made him very frightened, and he stayed quietly inside the cave. As he grew bigger, he became less afraid. Whenever his mother went out, he used to peep out after her. Finally one day he came right out of the cave.

There was a large ox eating grass nearby. The little goat had never seen such a big animal. But seeing its horns he decided that it was a goat like himself, and had grown so big by having very good things to eat. So he went up to the ox and said, 'I say, what do you eat?'

'I eat grass,' said the ox.

The little goat said, 'But my mother also eats grass, and she hasn't grown as big as you."

'I eat much more grass than your mother does,' said the ox, 'and much better grass too.'

'Where is this grass?' asked the little goat.'

'Over in that forest,' said the ox.

'You must take me there!' said the little goat. So the ox took him along.

Inside the forest, the grass was very fine. The little goat ate as much as his stomach would hold; and when he had finished he felt so weighed down that he couldn't move any more.

When it began to get dark, the ox said, 'Now let's go home.'

But how could the little goat go home? He couldn't even move.

'You go; I'll go tomorrow,' he said.

So the ox went away. The little goat found a hole and got inside it.

This hole belonged to a jackal, who had been invited to his uncle the tiger's house for supper. When he returned late at night he saw that some kind of animal had got inside his hole. The little goat was black, so the jackal couldn't see him well in the dark. He decided that it must be some kind of monster or devil. So he asked fearfully, 'Who is that inside the hole?'

The little goat was very clever; he said —

> My beard is long,
> I shake it to and fro,
> My name is Narahari Das the strong
> And I swallow fifty tigers at one go!

'Help!' yelled the jackal, and he took to his heels. He was in such a panic that he didn't draw breath till he was right back at the tiger's place.

The tiger was very surprised to see him and asked, 'What is it, nephew? You've only just gone; why have you come rushing back like this?'

'Uncle,' panted the jackal, 'a terrible thing has happened; a monster called Narahari Das is in my hole. He says he swallows fifty tigers at one go!'

The tiger was furious at this and said, 'So! He's as boastful as that, is he! Come along, nephew. We'll see how he swallows fifty tigers at one go!'

'I can't go back there,' said the jackal. 'If I go there, and he comes out to snap us up, you'll be able to get away in two leaps. But I can't escape like that, and the beast will catch me and eat me.'

'What do you mean?' said the tiger. 'I shall never run off without you.'

13

'All the same,' said the jackal, 'tie me to your tail before we go.' So the tiger tied the jackal firmly to his tail, and the jackal thought, 'Now my uncle the tiger won't be able to run off without me.'

The two of them arrived at the jackal's hole tied together in this way. The little goat saw them coming and said to the jackal —

> You stupid fool — be gone, be gone.
> I gave you the money for tigers ten,
> But you've roped up the tail of only one!

The tiger jumped out of his skin with fright. He was sure that the jackal had tricked him and brought him to give to Narahari Das to eat. He didn't wait any longer, but leapt

forty feet in one bound and ran off with the jackal still tied to him. The poor jackal was knocked about on the ground, torn by thorns, battered against fences, till he was half dead. 'Ow! uncle, Ow! uncle,' he screamed; but the tiger thought he was screaming because Narahari Das was behind them, so he ran even faster. He ran on all night like this until he was tired out.

In the morning the little goat went home.

The jackal had had a terrible time that night. From then on he was so angry with the tiger that he never ever forgave him.

5 Uncle Tiger and his Nephew the Jackal

'YOU WAIT, UNCLE,' thought the jackal, 'I'll get my own back on you!' He hadn't gone back to his old hole, for fear of Narahari Das, but had found a new one.

Near this hole there was a well.

One day the jackal caught sight of a mat lying on the river-

bank, and dragged it home, where he spread it neatly over the mouth of the well. Then he went to the tiger and said, 'Uncle, won't you come and see my new house?' The tiger came along to see it straight away. The jackal showed him the mat spread out over the well and said, 'Won't you sit down for a bit, uncle, and have something to eat?'

The tiger was delighted at the mention of food, and bounding on to the mat promptly fell into the well. 'Drink all you want, uncle,' said the jackal. 'You needn't leave a drop!'

But there wasn't enough water in the well to drown the tiger. At first he was terrified, but in the end he managed to clamber out. 'Where is that rascal of a nephew?' he growled. 'He won't get away with this.' But the jackal had fled far away by now, and the tiger couldn't find him anywhere.

The jackal was now too frightened of the tiger to go about looking for food, let alone return to his home. Whenever the tiger saw him in the distance he chased after him, and the poor jackal was soon half-dead from hunger and exhaustion.

'I'll die anyway if I go on like this,' he thought, 'so I might as well go to the tiger and see if I can calm him down.'

So along he went to see his uncle. Even while he was still some way from the tiger's lair he began to greet him and call out, 'Uncle, uncle.'

'Is that you, nephew?' said the tiger in astonishment.

At once the jackal ran up to him, bowed low before him and said, 'Uncle, you know how I love you. I can't bear to see you going to such trouble to find me. Please kill me here in your own house.'

The tiger was most embarrassed at what the jackal said. He didn't kill him; he just said crossly, 'You good-for-nothing wretch, why did you put me down that well?'

'Heaven forbid,' said the jackal, biting his tongue and covering his ears. 'Would I ever do such a thing? The ground there is very soft; you jumped on to it and it gave way beneath you. You're such a huge, fine figure of a tiger!'

When he heard this the stupid tiger smiled and said, 'That's

17

right, nephew, yes — I didn't realize what had happened at the time.'

So they were friendly once again.

One day after this the jackal was walking along the river when he saw a thirty foot long crocodile on a mudbank, basking in the sun. He hurried along to the tiger and said, 'Uncle, I've bought a boat. Come and see it.'

The stupid tiger went and jumped on to the crocodile, thinking it really was a boat. It immediately clamped him in its jaws and pulled him down into the water.

And the jackal went skipping and dancing back to his hole.

6 The Story of the Foolish Weaver and the Jackal

ONCE there was a foolish weaver. One day he went out with his scythe to cut paddy, and fell asleep in the middle of the field. When he woke and picked up his scythe again, he found that it was extremely hot.

The scythe had been heated by the sun, but the weaver thought it had caught a fever. He began to weep and howl, 'My scythe will die, my scythe will die!'

In the next field there was a farmer working. When he heard the weaver's howling he called, 'What's happened?'

'My scythe has caught a fever,' said the weaver.

The farmer laughed and said, 'Dip it into the water, and the fever will go.'

So the weaver dipped the scythe into the water, and was delighted to find that it cooled down.

A few days later the weaver's mother caught a fever. Everyone told him to call the doctor; but the weaver said, 'I know what to do.' He took his mother to the village pond and pressed her down under the water. The more the poor old lady struggled, the more the weaver pressed her down, saying, 'Wait, the fever is going.'

When the old lady stopped moving and struggling, he lifted her out and saw that she was dead. How the weaver cried his eyes out! For three days he neither ate nor left the pond to go home.

Now there was a jackal who was friendly with the weaver. When he saw the weaver weeping he came and said, 'Don't cry, my friend; I'll get you the king's daughter for your wife.'

The weaver dried his eyes when he heard this, and went home. Every day from then on he would say to the jackal, 'Hey, aren't you going to do as you said?'

The jackal said, 'I always do what I say I will do. First let me see if you can weave some really fine cloth.' So for two months the weaver did nothing but weave cloth. Then the jackal told him to have a good bath, soaping himself all over, while he set off to ask the king for the princess's hand.

When the jackal came before the king, he had a pen stuck behind his ear, a turban tied round his head, shoes on his feet, a shirt and a robe on his body, and an umbrella under his arm; and the king thought, 'This is a very learned person.' He asked, 'What have you come for, scholar jackal?'

'I have come to find out if you will give our Rajah your daughter's hand in marriage,' said the jackal.

Rajah was the weaver's name, so the jackal wasn't lying; but it is also a word meaning 'king', and the king thought that he meant a real-life king. 'What is your Rajah like?' he asked eagerly.

The jackal said—

> In looks our Rajah's very fine;
> His room is full of bright moonshine.
> In scholarship he can command
> All that his brains can understand.
> One blow from him can knock down ten;
> His power feeds and dresses men.

The weaver was indeed a very handsome man, which is why the jackal said, 'In looks our Rajah's very fine'.

Because there was no thatch on his house, the moonlight used to shine in; so the jackal said, 'His room is full of bright moonshine'. But the king thought that this described a shining and glittering palace like his own.

The weaver had no brains, and couldn't read or write. This is why the jackal said, 'In scholarship he can command all that his brains can understand'. But the king thought he meant that he was very clever, and a very good scholar.

'One blow from him can knock down ten' was true, too. But the jackal didn't mean ten men, he meant ten rice-plants; for the weaver was also a farmer, and used to cut paddy with his scythe. The king, however, thought that the weaver must be a mighty warrior, who could kill ten men with one blow.

The weaver grew rice and wove cloth, and people used to eat his rice and wear his cloth. So the jackal said, 'His power feeds and dresses men'. But the king thought that the weaver was rich enough to feed and dress lots of poor people.

So the king was very pleased and gave the jackal a present of a thousand silver coins, saying, 'I couldn't marry my daughter to any man better than this. Bring your Rajah here, and we'll

21

hold the wedding in eight days' time.'

The jackal took the bag of money under his arm, and went skipping and dancing back to the weaver. When he got to him he saw that he was still weaving cloth. In two months he had woven so much cloth that he had enough to dress every single one of the villagers.

The jackal gave each of the villagers two coins from the money-bag and one piece of cloth, saying, 'In eight days' time, our friend the weaver will be married to the king's daughter. You are all invited.'

They were all very pleased to hear this. The weaver may have been stupid, but he was a good man and everyone liked him.

Then the jackal went to all the other jackals and said, 'Brothers, you are invited to the wedding of a friend of mine. You've been asked to sing songs.' 'Yes, yes, we'll go,' howled the jackals.

Then the jackal went to the frogs and said, 'Brothers, a friend of mine is getting married, and you are invited. You've been asked to sing songs.' 'Yes, yes, we'll go,' croaked the frogs.

Then the jackal went to the mynah-birds and said, 'Brothers, a friend of mine is getting married, and you are invited. You've been asked to sing songs.' 'Yes, yes, we'll go,' shrilled the mynah-birds.

Then the jackal went to the tree-pies, the doves, the crow-pheasants, the fishing-eagles, the cuckoos, the peacocks and the brain-fever birds, and invited them in the same way. They all said, 'Yes, yes, we'll go.'

It took seven days for all this inviting to be finished, and the wedding was fixed for the evening of the following day. The jackal hired beautiful clothes for his friend, and when he had dressed him in them the weaver began to feel he really was a great Rajah. All those the jackal had invited came along too. When it was time to go, the jackal took them all off to the king's palace.

When they were a couple of miles away from the palace,

the jackal called everyone and said, 'Brothers, over there are the lights of the king's palace. From now on you must proceed very slowly. I shall run on ahead meanwhile to give the king news of our arrival.'

'All right,' said all the birds and animals.

'Just sing together once before I go,' said the jackal. 'Let's see how strong your voices are.' Immediately five thousand jackals began to howl, 'Hooya, hooya, hooya!'

Twelve thousand frogs went, 'Crawk, crawk, creeca, creeca!'

Seven thousand mynah-birds went, 'Pretty boy, pretty boy, pretty boy!'

Two thousand tree-pies went, 'Chincha-chincha, chanch, chanch, chincha!'

Four thousand doves went 'Cooroo, cooroo, cooroo!'

Three thousand crow-pheasants went, 'Poot, poot, poot, poot, poot, poot!'

Nineteen hundred fishing-eagles went, 'Hong-ah, hong-ah, hong-ah, oho, ho ho ho!'

And the cuckoos, peacocks and brain-fever birds all joined in and went on and on making their own sounds.

You would need to have been there to know just what all this sounded like. When the courtiers heard it approaching they began to quake with fright: and when the jackal came to announce the bridegroom's arrival, the king very nervously enquired, 'Scholar jackal, what is that din?'

'That is the noise of our musicians and attendants,' said the jackal.

The king was most alarmed. He had no idea where he would seat so many people, or what he would feed them with. 'Dear me, what am I to do?' he said to the jackal.

'What is there to fear, Your Majesty?' said the jackal. 'I'll go and send them all back at once. I'll just bring our Rajah to you.'

The king was very relieved, and gave the jackal a present of five thousand silver coins. The jackal returned to the birds and animals and bought a great quantity of fish and sugared rice, which he scattered over the fields. 'Eat, brothers,' he said; and the jackals, frogs and birds began to gobble it up. The jackal also gave the villagers who had come their fill of sweets, and sent them home. Then he brought the weaver to the king. On the way he warned him, 'Be careful! Don't say a word, or you won't be married.'

When the courtiers saw the bridegroom they were more pleased than I can say! There was only one thing that worried them: the groom was very handsome, but why didn't he speak?

'His mother has recently died,' said the jackal, 'and he has been struck dumb with sorrow.' 'Ah,' they all said. But the real fact was that the weaver would have been found out if he had spoken, and this is why the jackal had told him not to.

When it was time to eat, the weaver was given rice on a gold plate and various vegetables and sweets on a hundred gold dishes. One by one he lifted them up and smelt them. Because he'd never seen food like this before, he poured them all on to his rice — sweets, sauces and savories all together — and mixed them into a mess. In the end he could only eat a little bit, and tied up the rest into his robe.

Everyone asked the jackal, 'Why is your Rajah like this? Has he never eaten in his life before?'

But the jackal winked and whispered in their ears, 'He takes only one helping of food at a meal, and ties up whatever is left on his plate into his robe, so that he can give it to the poor. Call a poor man.'

Then he took the robe with the food tied in it from off the weaver's back, and gave it to the poor man.

When it was time to go to bed the weaver had a lot of trouble. There was a mosquito net hung round the ivory bedstead; but the poor man had never seen either a bedstead or a mosquito net before.

First of all he got underneath the bed, but when he saw there was no bedding there he came out. Then he looked all

24

round the four sides of the mosquito net, and finding no entrance said, 'I see now that they have made a room within a room, and the door must be in the roof.'

So he climbed up the posts of the bed and tried to get on to the roof of the mosquito net. It all came crashing down! The weaver burst into tears and said, 'I used to cut paddy and weave cloth and I was all right. Now I've married a princess and I've nearly broken my back.'

Fortunately there was no one else there; only the princess herself, and the jackal sitting outside. The princess burst into tears too, and was furious with the jackal for arranging such a marriage. But she had the sense not to let anyone else know what had happened.

The next day, at the princess's request, the jackal went to the king and said, 'Your Majesty, your son-in-law has asked if he can take your daughter on a tour of various countries. He begs leave of absence.'

The king was happy to grant them leave, and supplied them with money and servants. So the king's daughter took the weaver to another country, and engaged famous teachers to teach him all kinds of arts and sciences. In two or three years the weaver had become a great scholar and warrior.

Then news came that the king had died, and as he had no son he had left his son-in-law the throne. So everyone was very happy.

25

7 The Story of the Hunchbacked Old Woman

THERE WAS ONCE a hunchbacked old woman. She leant on a stick as she walked along, hunched forward, head bobbing. She had two dogs—one called Ranga and the other Bhanga.

This old woman wanted to visit her grand-daughter, so she said to the two dogs, 'You stay at home, and don't go wandering about anywhere.'

'We won't,' said Ranga and Bhanga. So the old woman set out, hunched forward over her stick, and her head kept bobbing away. She went a small part of the way like this.

Then a jackal saw her. 'Aha,' he said to himself, 'there's that hunchbacked

26

old woman. Old woman, I'm going to eat you up!'

'Wait a bit,' said the old woman, 'let me first go to my grand-daughter's house and get fat. Then you can eat me. If you eat me now you'll get nothing but skin and bone: what else is there on my body?'

'All right,' said the jackal, 'come when you're fat, and then I'll eat you.' And he went away.

The old woman set off again, hunched forward over her stick, with her head bobbing away. She went a little further like this.

Then a tiger saw her. 'Aha,' he said to himself, 'there's that hunchbacked old woman. Old woman, I'm going to eat you up!'

'Wait a bit,' said the old woman, 'let me first go to my grand-daughter's house and get fat. Then you can eat me. If you eat me now you'll get nothing but skin and bone: what else is there on my body?'

'All right,' said the tiger, 'come when you're fat, and then I'll eat you.' And he went away.

The old woman set off again, hunched forward over her stick, with her head bobbing away. She went a little further like this.

Then a bear saw her. 'Aha,' he said to himself, 'there's that hunchbacked old woman. Old woman, I'm going to eat you up!'

'Wait a bit,' said the old woman, 'let me first go to my grand-daughter's house and get fat. Then you can eat me. If you eat me now you'll get nothing but skin and bone: what else is there on my body?'

'All right,' said the bear, 'come when you're fat, and then I'll eat you.' And he went away.

The old woman went on a little further until she arrived at her grand-daughter's house. There she ate and ate so many sweets and curds that she grew fatter than I can say! If she had got any fatter she would have burst.

'I must go home, my dear,' she said to her grand-daughter,

'but I shan't be able to walk any more now. I shall have to roll along. And a bear, a tiger and a jackal are lying in wait for me on the path. As soon as they see me they'll pounce and snap me up. What do you think I should do?'

'What are you afraid of, Granny?' said her grand-daughter. 'I can stuff you into this hollow gourd-skin — then the tiger and bear won't know you're there and won't be able to eat you either.'

So she stuffed the old lady into the gourd-skin, giving her pressed rice and tamarinds to eat on the journey, and with a 'Heave-ho!' and a good strong push she set the gourd trundling forward like a cart.

As the gourd rolled along the old woman chanted from inside —

> *Roll, gourd, roll away,*
> *This is the way to go!*
> *With rice to eat and pips to throw*
> *The fat old woman has gone a long way —*
> *Roll, gourd, roll away.*

In the middle of the path the bear was waiting with his mouth open, ready to eat the old woman. He couldn't see any old women around; all he saw was the gourd rolling along. He turned it over: this was no old woman nor anything worth eating! And when a voice seemed to call from inside, 'The fat old woman has gone a long way', he thought that she must have escaped. So with a snort he gave the gourd a good thump and set it trundling forward again like a cart.

As the gourd rolled along the old woman chanted from inside —

> *Roll, gourd, roll away,*
> *This is the way to go!*
> *With rice to eat and pips to throw*
> *The fat old woman has gone a long way —*
> *Roll, gourd, roll away.*

The Story of the Hunchbacked Old Woman

A little further on the tiger was waiting to eat the old woman. He didn't see her; all he saw was the gourd rolling along He turned it over: this was no old woman nor anything worth eating! And when a voice seemed to call from inside, 'The fat old woman has gone a long way', he also thought that she must have escaped. So with a snarl he gave the gourd a good thump and set it trundling along like a cart.

As the gourd rolled along the old woman chanted from inside —

> Roll, gourd, roll away,
> This is the way to go!
> With rice to eat and pips to throw
> The fat old woman has gone a long way —
> Roll, gourd, roll away.

Further on still the jackal was sitting in the middle of the path. When he saw the gourd he said, 'Ha! who ever heard of a gourd speaking? I must see what there is inside it.' So the rascally animal kicked the gourd to pieces and said, 'Old woman, now I shall eat you.'

'By all means eat me!' said the old woman. 'What else do you think I've come for? But wouldn't you like me to sing you a couple of songs first?'

'That's not a bad idea,' said the jackal. 'I do a bit of singing myself.'

'Fine,' said the old woman. 'I'll just climb up on to this mound and then I'll sing.' So she climbed on to the mound and sang out at the top of her voice, 'Ranga, Bhanga, come on, boys, come!'

At once the old woman's two dogs came bounding up to her, and one seized the jackal's neck while the other hung on to his haunches. How they pulled and pulled! The jackal's neck broke, his tongue lolled out, and his life left him — but they just went on pulling and pulling.

8 The Story of the Old Woman and her Rice

THERE WAS ONCE an old woman who was very fond of stale rice steeped in water overnight. But a thief came every night and ate up the rice, so the old woman went to complain to the king.

As she hobbled along, leaning on her stick, she passed a pond. A spiked catfish saw her and asked, 'Where are you going, old woman?'

'Thieves come and eat my rice,' she replied, 'so I am on my way to the king to complain.'

'Pick me up on your way back,' said the catfish, 'and I'll help you.'

'I will,' said the old woman.

A little later she passed under a wood-apple tree. One of the fruits fell on to the ground before her and asked, 'Where are you going, old woman?'

'Thieves come and eat my rice,' she re-

30

plied, 'so I am on my way to the king to complain.'

'Pick me up on your way back,' said the wood-apple, 'and I'll help you.'

'I will,' said the old woman.

A little later she noticed a small cow-pat by the side of the path. 'Where are you going, old woman?' asked the cow-pat.

'Thieves come and eat my rice,' she replied, 'so I am on my way to the king to complain.'

'Pick me up on your way back,' said the cow-pat, 'and I'll help you.'

'I will,' said the old woman.

A little further on the old woman saw a razor lying by the path. 'Where are you going, old woman!' asked the razor.

'Thieves come and eat my rice,' she replied, 'so I am on my way to the king to complain.'

'Take me along with you on your way back,' said the razor, 'and I'll help you.'

'I will,' said the old woman.

When the old woman reached the king's palace she found that he wasn't there. So she couldn't make her complaint.

On her way home she remembered the razor and the cow-pat, the wood-apple and the catfish. She picked them all up and put them in her basket.

As soon as she reached the yard of her house, the razor said to her, 'Put me down here on the grass.' So the old woman put the razor down on the grass.

And as she entered the house the cow-pat said, 'Leave me here on the threshold.' So the old woman left the cow-pat on the threshold.

And as soon as she was inside the house the wood-apple said, 'Put me inside the oven.' So the old woman put it there.

Finally the catfish said, 'Put me into your pan of rice.' And the old woman did as she was asked.

When it was dark the old woman had her supper and lay down to sleep.

In the middle of the night the thief came. Of course he

didn't know about the traps that had been laid for him. He went straight to the pan of rice and put his hand into it. The catfish inside the pan jabbed the poor man so fiercely with its spike that his eyes watered.

Weeping from his wound, the thief went across to the oven, where the wood-apple was. He put his hand into the oven to warm his sore fingers, and at once the fruit burst and its hard shell flew up into his eyes and face in fragments.

Nearly mad with fear and pain, he dashed for the door, trod on the cow-pat, slipped and sat down heavily in it with a thump.

The cow-pat covered him with filth, so he went to the grass to wipe himself. But that was where the razor was, and it cut him to shreds. All he could do now was scream and shout, 'Aaaahhh! Ooouch! Help!'.

When the villagers heard him they came rushing out, crying, 'It's the thief! Catch the thief! Kill him! Tear off his ears!'

And the thief got the hiding of his life.

9 The Story of the Sparrow
and the Crow

A SPARROW and a crow knew each other very well.

In the yard of a house, on a palm-leaf mat, rice and chillies had been put out in the sun. 'My friend,' said the sparrow to the crow, 'if you eat the chillies and I eat the rice, which of us will be the first to finish?'

'I shall,' said the crow.

'No, I shall,' said the sparrow.

'What happens if you don't finish first?' asked the crow.

'If I don't finish the rice first,' said the sparrow, 'you can peck out my heart. And what happens if you don't finish first?'

'You can peck out my heart,' said the crow.

So the two of them began to eat the rice and the chillies. The sparrow pecked up the grains of rice one by one, and the

crow scooped up the chillies one by one. Before long the crow had finished all the chillies, while the sparrow hadn't even eaten a quarter of the rice.

'Well, my friend,' said the crow, 'how about it?'

'What can I say?' said the sparrow. 'If, although you're my friend, you want to peck out my heart, you can go ahead. But go and wash your beak first — you eat such dirty things.'

'I'll go and wash it at once,' said the crow, and he went to the river to wash his beak.

But the river said to him, 'Don't you dip your dirty beak into my clean water. Take some of the water and then wash.'

'All right,' said the crow, 'I'll go and get a water-pot.' And he went to the potter and said —

> Potter, potter, give me a pot
> To hold the water to wash my beak
> Before I peck out the sparrow's heart.

'I haven't got a pot,' said the potter. 'But bring me some clay and I'll make you one.' So the crow went to the buffalo to ask him for his horn so that he could use it to dig up the clay, and said —

> Buffalo, buffalo, give me your horn
> To dig the clay to make the pot
> To hold the water to wash my beak
> Before I peck out the sparrow's heart.

But the buffalo butted at him angrily and chased him away. So the crow went to the dog and said —

> Dog, dog, kill the buffalo
> To get the horn to dig the clay to make the pot
> To hold the water to wash my beak
> Before I peck out the sparrow's heart.

'Bring me some milk first,' said the dog. 'I'll kill the buffalo when I've built up my strength.' So the crow went to the cow and said —

34

> Cow, cow, give me some milk
> To feed to the dog to give him strength
> To kill the buffalo to get the horn
> To dig the clay to make the pot
> To hold the water to wash my beak
> Before I peck out the sparrow's heart.

'Bring me some grass,' said the cow, 'and then I'll give you milk.'

So the crow went to the field and said —

> Field, field, give me some grass
> To feed to the cow to get some milk
> To feed to the dog to give him strength
> To kill the buffalo to get the horn
> To dig the clay to make the pot
> To hold the water to wash my beak
> Before I peck out the sparrow's heart.

'There's plenty of grass,' said the field, 'help yourself.' So the crow went to the blacksmith and said —

> Blacksmith, blacksmith, give me a scythe
> To cut some grass to feed to the cow
> To get some milk to feed to the dog
> To give him strength to kill the buffalo to get the horn
> To dig the clay to make the pot
> To hold the water to wash my beak
> Before I peck out the sparrow's heart.

'I've no fire,' said the blacksmith. 'Bring some fire and I'll make you a scythe.' So the crow went back to the house where he lived and said to the householder —

Master of the house, give me some fire
To make a scythe to cut some grass
To feed to the cow to get some milk
To feed to the dog to give him strength
To kill the buffalo to get the horn
To dig the clay to make the pot
To hold the water to wash my beak
Before I peck out the sparrow's heart.

The householder brought the crow a pan of embers and said, 'How will you carry them?'

The foolish crow spread out his wings and said, 'Tip them out on to my wings.'

The householder tipped the embers out on to the crow's wings, and the silly creature was burnt to death. So he didn't peck out the sparrow's heart after all.

10 The Story of the Sparrows and the Tiger

ONCE there was a cooking-pot hanging in the corner of the house, and a sparrow and his wife lived inside it.

One day the sparrow said, 'Wife, I wish I had some sweet cakes to eat.'

'Bring me the ingredients for sweet cakes,' said his wife, 'and I'll make some.'

'What do you need?' asked the sparrow.

'I need flour,' she replied, 'and treacle and bananas and milk, and firewood.'

'All right,' said the sparrow, 'I'll bring you everything.' So he went to the forest and started to snap off the tiniest, driest twigs that were on the trees.

Now there was a huge tiger in the forest who was friendly towards the sparrow. When he heard the noise of twigs breaking he said, 'You're snapping off twigs, are you, my friend?'

'Yes,' said the sparrow.

'What do you want the twigs for?' asked the tiger.

'I want some firewood,' said the sparrow, 'so that my wife can make some sweet cakes.'

'I've never eaten sweet cakes,' said the tiger. 'You must give me some.'

'Only if you bring us all the ingredients,' said the sparrow.

'What ingredients do you want?' asked the tiger.

'We want flour,' said the sparrow, 'and treacle and bananas and milk and butter and pots and pans and firewood.'

'All right,' said the tiger, 'you go home and I'll bring you everything.' So the sparrow went home, and the tiger went loping off to the market. When he got there all he had to do was roar — and at once all the stall-holders shrieked, 'Help, help! Tiger! Run, run!' and fled wildly, leaving everything behind them. The tiger went round all the stalls to collect flour, treacle, bananas, milk, butter, pots and pans and firewood, and delivered them to the sparrows' home.

Then the sparrow's wife made some excellent sweet cakes, and the two of them ate as many as they could hold. When they had finished they laid out a few cakes for the tiger on a leaf on the ground, and settled down quietly in their cooking-pot.

When the tiger came and saw the cakes he sat down to eat.

As he put the first one into his mouth he said, 'Ah! delicious!'

As he tried the second he said, 'No, this isn't so good. It's nothing but flour.'

As he tried the third one he said, 'Ugh! this is just bran and ashes. My friend, what have you given me?'

As he tried the fourth cake he roared, 'Eeeraah! what a stink! They've put cow-dung into it! That miserable sparrow is a rogue and a villain!'

Meanwhile inside the cooking-pot the sparrow was

screwing up his face and saying, 'Wife, I'm going to sneeze.'

'Ssh, ssh,' hissed his wife in a fluster, 'you can't sneeze now — we'll be in terrible trouble.'

The sparrow managed to keep quiet. But a little later he was screwing up his face for a violent sneeze. His wife did all she could to stop him, but he just couldn't hold it back.

After eating another foul cake the tiger bellowed, 'Urraah! Urraah! This is nothing more than cow-dung — that's all they've given me. If I get within reach of that sparrow I'll chew him up and swallow him.'

When he had put the last cake into his mouth he started to retch and groan, and that was when the sparrow sneezed with a tremendous 'Aah-choo!' The tiger jumped so violently in alarm at the noise that he caught the string that held the cooking-pot, and the sparrows clattered down with it on to his neck.

The tiger didn't know what was happening — whether thunder had struck or the sky had fallen. He dashed from the spot in terror, tail between his legs, and didn't stop until he had reached his lair.

11 The Wicked Tiger

NEXT to the lion-gateway of the king's palace there was a huge tiger in an iron cage. The tiger used to go down on his knees to all the people who passed to and fro in front of the palace and say, 'Won't you please open the door of the cage for me just this once, kind sirs?' 'You must be joking,' they replied. 'If we open the door for you you'll break our necks.'

Meanwhile one day there was a lavish feast at the palace. Learned men came flocking to attend it. Amongst them was a Brahmin who looked very kind and innocent. The tiger started to bow and scrape before him, and the Brahmin said, 'Ah, this is a very well-mannered tiger! What do you want, my son?'

The tiger clasped his paws together and said, 'Please be so good as to open the door of this cage for me. I implore you on my bended knees.'

The Brahmin was such a kind-hearted man that he quickly did what the tiger asked and opened the cage-door.

Then the good-for-nothing tiger came grinning out of the cage and said, 'Sir, I'm going to eat you up!'

Anyone else would have fled instantly. But this Brahmin didn't know how to flee. 'I've never heard anything like it!' he said in great dismay. 'I've done you such a favour and now you say you're going to eat me! Surely people don't do such things, do they?'

'Indeed they do,' said the tiger. 'They do it all the time.'

'That can't be so,' said the Brahmin. 'Come on, let's find three witnesses and see what they say.'

'All right', said the tiger. 'If the witnesses agree with you, I'll release you and go on my way. But if they say that I'm right, I'll catch you and eat you up.'

The two of them went into the fields to look for witnesses. Between two of the fields the farmers had banked up some earth to make a small raised path. The Brahmin pointed to the path and said, 'This can be one of my witnesses.'

'Very well,' said the tiger, 'ask him what he thinks.'

So the Brahmin called to the path, 'Hey, my friend, tell me what you think: if I do good to someone, does he do me harm in return?'

'Yes indeed, sir,' said the path. 'Look at what happens to me. By lying between two farmers' fields I do them a great service. Neither of them can take away the other's land; the water in one field cannot go into the other. I do them this service, but the wretches hack me with their ploughs to make their fields bigger.'

'You hear what he says, sir,' said the tiger, 'how harm is done in return for good?'

'Wait,' said the Brahmin, 'I still have another two witnesses to come.'

41

'All right, let's find them,' said the tiger.

In the middle of a field there was a banyan tree. The Brahmin pointed it out and said, 'This can be my second witness.'

'Very well,' said the tiger, 'ask him, and let's see what he says.'

So the Brahmin called to the banyan tree, 'My friend, you are very old, and have seen and heard much. Tell me, if someone does a good turn can he receive a bad turn back?'

'That's the first thing that happens to me,' said the banyan tree. 'People sit in my shade to get cool, yet they jab me to get my sap for glue. They even tear off my leaves to catch the sap in. Look at this — one of my branches has just been broken off.'

'Well, sir,' said the tiger, 'you hear what he says.'

The Brahmin was now in some difficulty and couldn't quite think of what to say. But at that moment a jackal happened to be passing. The Brahmin pointed to the jackal and said, 'He can be my third witness. Let's see what he says.'

So he called out to the jackal, 'Jackal, sir, stop a minute and be a witness for me.'

The jackal stopped, but wasn't keen to come closer. He answered from a distance, 'What a strange request! How can I be your witness?'

'Tell me,' said the Brahmin, 'do people harm those who have done them favours?'

'Who has done the favour, and who has done the harm?' asked the jackal. 'If you tell me, then I can give you my opinion.'

'This tiger was in a cage,' said the Brahmin, 'and a Brahmin was walking along the path —'

'This is very complicated,' interrupted the jackal. 'I shan't be able to say anything unless I see the cage and the path.'

So they all had to go back to see the cage. When the jackal had paced all round it, examining it closely from all sides, he said, 'All right, I've got the cage and path straight. Now tell me what happened.'

'The tiger was in the cage,' said the Brahmin, 'and a Brahmin was walking along the path —'

At once the jackal stopped him and said, 'Wait a minute — don't go so fast. I want to get this first bit clear. What were you saying? The tiger was a Brahmin, and the path was walking through the cage?'

The tiger burst out laughing when he heard this and said, 'What an ass you are! The tiger was in the cage and the Brahmin was walking along the path.'

'Hang on,' said the jackal, 'the Brahmin was in the cage, and the tiger was walking along the path —'

'No, you fool, not that,' said the tiger. 'The tiger was in the cage and the Brahmin was walking along the path.'

'I can see that this is going to be a very confusing story,' said the jackal. 'I can't follow it at all. What did you say? The tiger was in the Brahmin, and the cage was walking along the path?'

'Never have I met such an idiot!' bellowed the tiger. 'It was the tiger who was in the cage, and the Brahmin was walking along the path.'

'It's no good,' said the jackal, scratching his head. 'I won't be able to understand such a difficult story.'

The tiger lost his temper.

'You will have to understand it,' he roared. 'Look, I was inside this cage — look — like this —' As he spoke he got into the cage. The jackal shut the door and drew the bolt. Then he said to the Brahmin, 'Good sir, now I understand everything. If you want to hear my opinion, it is this: you should not do favours for the wicked. The tiger was right: bad is often done in return for good. Run away quickly now — the feast in the palace is not over yet.' And the jackal went off to the forest, while the Brahmin went to join the feast.

12 The Tiger and the Palanquin

THE TIGER is the jackal's uncle, and so they know each other very well.

One day the jackal invited the tiger to dinner, but he didn't prepare any food for him. 'Sit down a minute, uncle,' said the jackal when the tiger arrived. 'I've invited two or three other guests—let me just go and call them.'

So the jackal went off, and didn't return home that night. The tiger waited for the whole night, and went home in the morning, cursing his nephew.

A few days later the tiger invited the jackal for dinner. When he arrived he gave him huge thick bones to eat, each as hard as iron. The poor jackal broke four teeth over them, but he couldn't crunch or chew them at all. The tiger loved eating bones like this. He cheerfully

ate his way through them all and said, 'Well, nephew, have you had enough to eat?'

'Yes, uncle,' said the jackal with a smile, 'I've eaten as well in your house as you did in mine.' But he was furious inside, and said to himself, 'I shan't come near here unless I can be revenged on the tiger; if I can't I shall never return to these parts.'

So the jackal left, and found a new place to live. This was in an area of sugar-cane fields. The jackal took to gorging himself on sugar-cane. Any that he couldn't eat he smashed and left.

'This is a fine thing,' said the farmers. 'Some wretched jackal must be smashing down our sugar-cane. We must deal with the villain.' So they laid a trap next to the field.

The trap was made like a small wooden hut. If any animal got inside it the door would shut by itself, and the animal would be caught.

The jackal smiled when he saw that the farmers had made the trap, and said to himself, 'For me or for uncle? A beautiful house like that would suit my uncle very well.'

Next day he went to the tiger and said, 'Uncle, an important invitation has come. The king's son is getting married, and I am to sing and you are to play at the wedding. There'll be no end of things to eat. A palanquin has been sent for us — will you come, uncle?'

'Will I come?' said the tiger. 'Do you think such an invitation can be refused? And they've even sent a palanquin for us!'

'Don't think it's any old palanquin,' said the jackal. 'You've never ridden in such a palanquin, uncle.' With talk such as this the two of them reached the edge of the sugar-cane field, where the trap stood. When the tiger saw the trap he said, 'Have they only sent the palanquin and no bearers?'

'If we sit down inside it,' said the jackal, 'the bearers will be along soon.'

'The palanquin has no rods,' said the tiger. 'How will the bearers carry it?'

45

'They'll bring the rods with them,' said the jackal. At this the tiger got inside the trap and at once the door slammed shut. Then the jackal said, 'Uncle, you've shut the door — how am I to get in now?'

'There's no need for you to come in,' said the tiger. 'This time I'll be happy to eat on my own.'

'Well said, uncle!' said the jackal. 'Eat your fill at the wedding. Don't stint yourself.'

And the jackal made his way back to his old home, chuckling as he went.

When the farmers came and saw that a splendid tiger was sitting in the trap, they were more delighted that I can say!

'Bring spades, bring spears, bring anything you can,' they called. 'There's a tiger in the trap. Come on everyone, wherever you are!'

Immediately everyone came running, and the tiger was killed.

13 Buddhur Bap

THERE WAS ONCE an old farmer called Buddhur Bap.

One year flocks of weaver-birds came to eat the paddy that was ripening in Buddhur Bap's field. So he made a large rattle and tried to scare away the birds with it. But the birds weren't bothered by the noise of the rattle, and Buddhur Bap grew very angry. 'You villains,' he said, 'if ever I catch you I'll give you such a crack-smack-thwack as you've never known!'

There is no such thing as a 'crack-smack-thwack': this was just the ugliest threat that Buddhur Bap could think of. Every day the weaver-birds came, and every day Buddhur Bap tried to drive them off and threatened them with crack-smack-thwacks.

One night a strange thing happened: a huge tiger came and slept in Buddhur Bap's field, and in the morning he was still too sleepy to leave.

Buddhur Bap came as before to scare away the weaver-birds, shaking his rattle and shouting, 'You villains, if ever I catch you I'll give you such a crack-smack-thwack as you've never known!'—and the tiger was very intrigued. 'Crack-smack-thwack?' he thought, 'Is this some kind of new invention? I've never heard of such a thing!' The more he thought about it, the more determined he became to see it. So he stealthily emerged from the paddy-field and called to Buddhur Bap, 'My friend, a word with you please.'

I don't need to tell you how alarmed Buddhur Bap was when he saw the tiger! But he was a very clever man, and controlled himself so well that the tiger didn't notice he was scared. 'What do you want, brother?' he replied.

'What was that you were saying,' said the tiger, 'about a crack-smack-thwack? You must show it to me.'

'I can't show it to you just like that,' said Buddhur Bap. 'Quite a few things are needed for it.'

'I'll bring you all you need,' said the tiger. 'I insist that you show it to me.'

'Very well,' said Buddhur Bap, 'bring me what I need and then I'll show it to you.'

'What do you want?' asked the tiger.

'I want a large, stout sack,' he replied, 'and a long piece of thick rope; and I also want a heavy club.'

'Is that all you want?' said the tiger. 'It won't take me long to get those.'

It happened to be market-day that morning. The tiger went and hid in a bush by the path to the market. Soon three rice-dealers came along the path, and the sacks that rice-dealers carry are always very large and strong.

The tiger waited in the bush till the rice-dealers were nearly opposite him, and then with a roar he leapt out into the middle of the path. The three men shrieked, dropped what they were carrying and ran off in all directions.

The tiger picked up the rice-sacks and brought them to Buddhur Bap. Then he went to find the rope.

He didn't have to go far for it. There were lots of cows tied to stakes in the fields, and when the tiger approached them they broke their tethers and ran away. He collected up the ropes and brought them to Buddhur Bap. Finally he went to find the club.

This he took from a troupe of wrestlers who were exercising with clubs. As soon as he appeared they took to their heels, yelling their heads off! The tiger picked up their biggest club, carried it in his mouth to Buddhur Bap and said, 'I've brought you what you wanted; now show me the crack-smack-thwack.'

'Very well,' said Buddhur Bap, 'the first thing is for you to get inside this sack.'

48

The tiger immediately crawled in. Buddhur Bap quickly closed up the mouth of the sack, and wound the rope round firmly. The tiger was now unable to move a muscle.

Then Buddhur Bap gripped the club with both hands and brought it down sharply on to the sack. 'What ever are you doing?' said the tiger, much surprised.

'What's the matter?' said Buddhur Bap. 'I'm showing you the crack-smack-thwack. You aren't afraid, are you?'

It is a shameful thing to admit to being afraid, so the tiger said, 'No.'

Buddhur Bap now began to give the sack great thumps with the club. For a long time the tiger kept silent, not wanting to disgrace himself by crying out. But he couldn't keep this up for ever, and after about twelve blows he started a terrible bellowing and roaring. Soon he could bellow no longer, and began to groan. But Buddhur Bap didn't let up at all: he went on thumping as hard as he could. At last, when nothing could be heard any more, he decided the tiger was dead. So he opened the sack, dumped the body by the edge of the field and went off home for a rest.

But the tiger wasn't dead. After lying for four or five hours as though he were, he sat up. His body ached all over and he had a fever, but his anger was so great that he didn't think about the pain. All he did was roll his eyes and bare his teeth and growl, 'That scoundrel Buddhur Bap! Wretch! Villain! You wait, I'll show you!'

Buddhur Bap turned pale when he heard the tiger roaring again. He bolted the door of his house and didn't stir for three days, while the tiger paced round and round outside, hurling abuse at him. In the end the tiger came up to the door and said, as politely and humanly as possible, 'Could you give me a light, sir? I want to smoke.'

Buddhur Bap could tell that, polite and human though these words were, the voice was still very like a tiger's — he would have to have a good look before giving anyone a light. So he peeped out through a crack in the door and — Help!

49

there was the tiger: no chance of his opening the door now! He started to wail and groan, and answered, 'I have a very bad fever, my friend. I can't open the door. But if you push your stick under the door I'll tie a light to it.'

How could a tiger have a stick? He pushed his tail under the door instead. At once Buddhur Bap cut it off with one sweep of his chopping knife.

With an ear-splitting roar, the tiger jumped as high as the roof of Buddhur Bap's house. Then he took to his heels, curling up what little tail he had left and howling.

But Buddhur Bap was still very frightened. He knew all the tigers would join forces to come and kill him. And indeed the very next day he saw over twenty tigers moving towards his

50

house. What could he do now? Behind the house there was a
tall tamarind tree. Buddhur Bap climbed into the tree and
waited.

There was a large cooking-pot tied to one of the branches,
and he hid behind it as he watched to see what the tigers
would do.

When the tigers reached the house, they saw Buddhur Bap
behind the cooking-pot. They cursed him, snarled at him and
threatened him in every way they could. But he sat there
quietly, holding on to the cooking-pot, and didn't say a
word.

The tigers now worked out a plan for catching Buddhur
Bap. One of the cleverest among them said, 'Let the biggest of
us squat down on the ground. The next biggest can climb on
to his shoulders, the next one climb on to his and so on. This
way we shall be able to reach high enough to grab the villain
and eat him.'

The biggest tiger of all was the one who had been battered
and had had his tail cut off by Buddhur Bap. It hurt him badly
to sit down, because his tail had still not healed. But the plan
wouldn't work if he didn't sit down, and so he would have to
somehow. He noticed a hole in the ground, and managed to
sit by sticking his tail-stump into it. The other tigers now
started to climb on top of him one by one.

They piled themselves up, one on top of another, until they
saw that they were almost level with Buddhur Bap. A little
higher and they'd catch him.

Buddhur Bap untied the cooking-pot and held it up ready
to break it on the topmost tiger's head. 'Take this before you
get me,' he shouted—but before he threw it, guess what
happened! There was a land-crab inside the hole where the
first tiger had stuck his stump. Attracted by the smell of the
wound, it had slowly crawled up and gripped the stump in its
two claws. 'Aahh! Urrr!' roared the tailless tiger when the
crab pinched him. 'Stop! Help me! Buddhur Bap above and
Buddhur Bap below too!' Then he leapt up, and the tigers on

top of him fell thudding to the ground in a heap. At that very moment Buddhur Bap sent the cooking-pot crashing down on the tailless tiger's back, shouting, 'Take that! Take that! And I hope it breaks your neck!'

Do you think the tigers stayed there after that? They ran away with their ears back and their tails between their legs. And they never came near Buddhur Bap's house again.

14 The Stupid Tiger

THERE WAS ONCE a jackal living near the king's palace. His hole was just behind the king's goat-pen.

The king's goats were very sleek and plump, and the jackal wished he could eat them. But he didn't dare go near them, because of the king's goat-herds.

One day the jackal started to dig from inside his hole, and burrowed his way right up into the goat-pen. But he didn't manage to eat any of the goats: the goat-herds were waiting there, and as soon as they saw the jackal they caught him. Then they tethered him to a stake and went off. 'Tomorrow we can show him to everyone and have some fun,' they said as they went, 'then we can kill him. But it's getting dark now.'

After the goat-herds had gone the jackal sat there with his head drooping. Then a tiger passed that way. He

53

was most surprised when he saw the jackal and said, 'What's this, nephew? What are you sitting here for?'

'I'm getting married,' said the jackal.

'But where's the bride?' asked the tiger, 'and where is everybody else?'

'The bride is a princess,' said the jackal. 'They've gone to fetch her.'

'Why are you tied up?' said the tiger.

'I don't want to get married,' said the jackal, 'so they have tied me up in case I run away.'

'Really?' said the tiger. 'You don't want to get married?'

'That's right, uncle,' said the jackal. 'I don't want to get married at all.'

The tiger was most excited when he heard this and said, 'Then why don't you tie me up in your place and escape?'

'Gladly!' said the jackal. 'If you'll untie me, I'll tie you up and leave you.'

The tiger was overjoyed. He immediately freed the jackal, and the jackal quickly tethered him firmly to the stake. 'One thing, uncle,' he said, 'when the bride's relatives arrive they will tease you and joke with you. Will you be offended?'

'Of course not,' said the tiger. 'Why should I be offended by that? I'm not such a fool.' So the jackal went off, grinning broadly; and the tiger began to think about when they would bring the bride.

In the morning the goat-herds came back. When the tiger saw them he thought to himself, 'These must be the bride's relatives. They will probably start teasing me in a minute, so I must laugh along with them.'

The goat-herds had come to kill the jackal, but now there was a tiger sitting there. At once a great commotion broke out. Some of the goat-herds wanted to run away, but the others stopped them. 'Can't you see that he's tied up?' they shouted. 'What is there to be afraid of? Go and fetch axes and spades and spears!'

Then one of them brought a large brick and hurled it at the tiger.

'Ha ha! Hee-hee, hee-hee!' laughed the tiger.

Another goat-herd thrust at him with a bamboo pole.

'Hah, hah! Hee-hee, hee-hee!' went the tiger.

Another jabbed him with a spear.

'Ah-ha-ha! Ho-ho, ho-ho, ho-ho!' went the tiger. 'I can see that you're my bride's relatives.'

Then they jabbed him with the spear again.

This time the tiger burst out in a terrible fury. 'Aaarugh!' he spluttered. 'I'm not going to make as rotten a marriage as this.' And he tore himself free from the ropes and went off to the forest.

In the forest there was a place where the woodcutters sawed up wood. The woodcutters had left a large log half-sawn, propping it open with a wedge. When the tiger got to the forest he saw that the jackal was taking a rest on top of this half-sawn log.

'Hello, uncle,' said the jackal when he saw him. 'How was the wedding?'

'No good, nephew,' said the tiger. 'They teased me so dreadfully that I came away.'

'You did well to do that,' said the jackal. 'Come now, let's sit down together and have a chat.'

The tiger jumped on to the log at exactly the place where it gaped most widely. His tail went into the gap and hung there.

The jackal decided it would be fun to remove the wedge from the log. So he distracted the tiger by keeping him talking about various things, and little by little shifted the wedge. He worked at it until one pull would be enough to release it so that the tiger's tail would be trapped. Then, shouting 'Help, uncle, help!' he toppled off the log, pulling out the wedge as he fell, and started to writhe on the ground.

You can imagine what happened to the tiger! When the log clamped shut on his tail he let out an almighty yell and jumped into the air. His tail was snapped right through into two pieces, and now the tiger began to roll around on the ground with the jackal.

'Help, help me, nephew,' screamed the tiger. 'My tail has been torn off!'

'Help, help me, uncle,' cried the jackal. 'My back is broken!'

Rolling around in this way, the two of them found themselves lying in a patch of wild yams. The tiger couldn't roll another inch, but there was nothing wrong with the wicked jackal — he'd tricked the tiger from beginning to end.

There were lots of frogs among the yams, and the jackal ate his fill of them as he lay there. The tiger was so distraught with pain that he didn't notice the frogs; so he hadn't anything to eat. 'What are you eating, nephew?' he asked the jackal.

'There's nothing to eat but these yams,' said the jackal. 'My stomach has become quite puffed out with them.'

The tiger started to chew away at the coarse, poisonous yams: what else could he do? And to his horror his throat and mouth began to swell.

'Have you eaten the yams, uncle?' asked the jackal when he noticed this.

'I've eaten some, nephew,' the tiger said, 'but my throat has swollen terribly. You say your stomach is puffed out, but why has my throat swollen like this?'

'Because I'm a jackal and you're a tiger — that's why,' said the jackal.

For sixteen days the tiger couldn't move because of the pain in his tail and throat. He nearly died from having nothing to eat for all this time.

Eventually he noticed that the jackal was now standing and walking quite normally. 'What's this, nephew?' he asked. 'How have you managed to get better?'

'I have taken a very good medicine, uncle,' replied the jackal. 'I chewed up my own paws, and I was cured at once. Then my paws grew again before my eyes.'

'Is that so?' said the tiger. 'But why didn't you tell me?'

'I didn't think you would be able to chew up your own

paws — that's why I didn't tell you,' said the jackal.

At this the tiger grew tremendously angry and roared, 'So you, a jackal, can do it, and I, a tiger, can't?'

'You broke off that fine marriage because you were scared of a bit of teasing,' said the jackal. 'How was I to know that you would be able to chew up your own paws?' 'You see if I can't,' bellowed the tiger. And he chewed up his own four paws.

Three or four days later the tiger died from his terrible wounds.

15 The Story of the Stupid Crocodile

A CROCODILE and a jackal went out to do some farming together. They decided to grow potatoes. Potatoes grow under the soil, but the stalks show on the surface; and nothing can be done with the stalks. The stupid crocodile didn't know this: he thought the potatoes grew on the stalks like fruit.

So in order to cheat the jackal he said, 'The top ends of the plants can be mine, and the bottom ends can be yours.'

'That's all right by me,' laughed the jackal.

When the potatoes had grown, the crocodile cut off all the stalks and took them home. But when he looked at them he saw that there wasn't a single potato there. And when he went back to the field he saw that the jackal had carried off all the potatoes by digging the soil. 'So that's how it is,' thought the crocodile. 'I've lost out badly this time; but we'll see what happens next time.'

The next thing they grew was rice. The crocodile was determined not to be fooled from now on; and right at the beginning he said to the jackal, 'This time I shan't take the top ends, my friend; you must give me the bottom ends.'

'That's all right by me,' laughed the jackal.

When the rice had grown, the jackal came and cut off the top ends of the plants where the grain was, and the crocodile felt very pleased with himself: he would get all the rice by digging the soil. What bad luck! When he dug the soil he found nothing there. All he got was the stubble.

The crocodile was furious now and said to himself, 'You miserable jackal, just you wait! I'll be even with you. I shan't let you take the top ends next time. I'll come and take them all.'

The third thing they grew was sugar-cane.

The crocodile had insisted beforehand that the top ends be given to him. So the jackal gave him the tops of the plants, took the sugary canes back to his home, and cheerfully sat down to eat them.

The crocodile brought home the top ends. But when he chewed them he found they were all salty—there was no sweetness in them at all—and he angrily threw them away. 'No, brother,' he said to the jackal, 'I shan't go farming with you any more. You're nothing but a cheat!'

16 The Scholar Jackal

THE CROCODILE saw that he wasn't keeping up with the jackal at all. 'He's very learned,' he thought to himself. 'That's why he can trick me the whole time. I'm ignorant, so I can't catch him out.' After thinking about this for a long time, the crocodile decided that if he sent his own seven sons to be taught by the jackal they would learn a great deal. So the next day he took them along to where the jackal lived. The jackal was sitting inside his hole eating crabs, and the crocodile called from outside, 'Scholar jackal, are you at home?'

The jackal came out and said, 'What is it, brother, what do you want?'

'Brother,' said crocodile, 'I have brought these seven sons of mine to you. If they grow up ignorant they won't be able to fend for themselves. Could you give them a few lessons?'

'Is that all you want?' said the jackal. 'I'll turn all seven into scholars in seven days.' So the crocodile left his seven children with the jackal and went away very happily.

Then the jackal took one of the young crocodiles aside and said —

Read, my little one:
A for apple,
B for baby,
C for CROCODILE!

And he killed it by breaking its neck, and swallowed it. When the crocodile came next day to see his children, the jackal brought them out of the hole one by one and showed them to him. When he came to the sixth, he showed it twice, and the stupid crocodile imagined that the seventh had been shown to him. Off he went, and at once the jackal took another of the young crocodiles aside and said —

Read, my little one:
A for apple,
B for baby,
C for CROCODILE!

And he killed it by breaking its neck, and swallowed it.

The crocodile came next day to see his children again, and the jackal brought them out of the hole one by one. When he came to the fifth, he showed it three times, and the crocodile went away happily. The jackal then ate another of the young crocodiles in the same way as before.

Every day he ate one of them like this, and the crocodile was tricked each time he came. Finally there was only one left, and it had to be shown seven times; and after the crocodile had gone the jackal gobbled up this one too. Now there were none left at all.

'What will you do now?' asked the jackal's wife. 'What will you show the crocodile when he comes? If he finds his children have gone, he'll eat us up.'

'He'll only eat us if he can catch us,' said the jackal. 'There's a very big forest over the river: come on, let's go there. The crocodile will never find us.'

So the jackal and his wife left their old hole and went off towards the forest.

A little later the crocodile arrived. 'Scholar jackal, scholar jackal,' he called, but there was no answer; and when he had a look inside the hole he found neither the jackal nor the jackal's wife — nothing but the scattered bones of his children.

Then he became very angry and started to rush around everywhere in search of the jackal. And when he got to the bank of the river he saw the jackal and his wife swimming across.

'Wait, you scoundrel!' he shouted, and leapt into the water. No animal can swim as fast under water as a crocodile can, and in no time at all he had snatched hold of the jackal's hind-leg in his jaws.

The jackal had just got his two front paws on to the river-bank and his wife had already climbed out. 'Wife, wife,' shouted the jackal when the crocodile caught hold of his leg, 'who's pulling at my stick? Someone seems to want to take it.'

When the crocodile heard this he thought, 'So I'm holding on to a stick instead of a leg! I must let go of it quickly and grab his leg.'

He therefore let go of the leg that he was holding, and at once the jackal leapt up on to the bank with one bound. He darted off into the forest, where no one could catch him.

After this the crocodile spent all his days looking for the jackal; but the jackal was so clever that he couldn't catch him. In the end, after a lot of thought, the crocodile worked out a plan.

One day the crocodile went and lay on a sand-bank with his legs spread out as though he were dead. The jackal and his wife had come to the sand-bank to eat turtles, and they saw how the crocodile was lying there. 'He's dead,' said the jackal's wife. 'Let's go and eat.' But the jackal said, 'Wait a minute, let's have a closer look.' He went a little closer to the crocodile and said loudly, 'No! This one has been dead for far too long. We can't eat such old meat. It ought still to be moving a bit if it's good to eat.' The crocodile thought, 'I'd better move a little bit, otherwise they won't try to eat me.' And he started to twitch the tip of his tail. The jackal laughed and said to his wife, 'Look at that, his tail's moving! You said he was dead!' And they didn't stay another moment. 'He's tricked me again,' said the crocodile to himself, 'but we'll see what happens next time.'

There was a place where the jackal used to drink every day.

62

The crocodile had noticed this, and went and hid in the water. He hoped that he would catch the jackal when he came to drink.

When the jackal came that day he couldn't see a single fish there. There were usually lots of fish swimming about. 'Well well,' thought the jackal, 'I wonder where all the fish have gone. I know, the crocodile's here!'

Then he said loudly, 'The water here is far too clear and calm. You oughtn't to drink unless there's a bit of movement in it. Come on, wife, let's find another place.'

The crocodile quickly began to stir up the water; and when the jackal saw this he ran away again, laughing merrily.

On another day the jackal came to eat crabs. The crocodile

was quietly lying in wait for him. 'There are no crabs here,' said the jackal. 'If there were you would see one or two of them floating.'

At once the crocodile floated the tip of his tail; and the jackal didn't go down to the water.

In the end the crocodile was very ashamed that the jackal had outwitted him so many times. How could he show his face any more? He went back to his home and stayed there.

17 The Tiger-eating Jackal Cubs

A JACKAL and his wife had three cubs, but nowhere to live.

'Where shall we put the cubs?' they thought. 'If we don't get a hole they'll be soaked in the rain and die.' After searching for a long time they found a hole, but they could see tiger-prints all round it. 'This is a tiger's hole, my dear,' said the jackal's wife. 'How can we live here?'

'We've searched for so long,' said the jackal, 'and this is the only hole we've found. We shall have to live here.'

'What shall we do if the tiger comes?' said his wife.

'You must pinch the cubs hard if he does,' said the jackal. 'They'll squeal, and I shall ask—why are they crying? And you will say—they want to eat tiger.'

'All right,' said his wife, 'I understand. That's fine.' She went happily into the hole, and they settled down there.

A few days passed, and then they saw the tiger approaching. At once the jackal's wife started to pinch her cubs sharply, and they squealed more than I can say!

'Why are the little ones crying?' asked the jackal in a very deep and ugly voice.

'They want to eat tiger, that's why they're crying,' said his wife, also in a deep voice.

The tiger was about to go into his hole, but when he heard the words 'They want to eat tiger', he stopped short. 'Good gracious,' he thought to himself, 'whatever can have got into my hole? They must surely be most dreadful monsters, otherwise would their young ones want to eat tiger?'

Then the jackal said, 'Where can we get more tigers? I've caught all that there were and given them to them.'

'It's no use saying that,' said his wife. 'The children won't stop squealing unless you find another one somehow.' And she pinched the cubs even harder. 'It's all right,' said the jackal. 'There's a tiger coming now. Give me my jimplong, and I'll ballyram him.'

There is no such thing as a jimplong, and ballyram doesn't mean anything either: they were all part of the jackal's trickery. But the tiger jumped out of his skin when he heard the words jimplong and ballyram. 'Heavens, I must get away at once,' he thought, 'or who knows what it will bring and what it will do to me!' And he didn't wait a moment longer. The jackal watched him as he raced off, bounding over bushes and thickets; and when the danger had passed, he and his wife breathed a long sigh of relief.

The tiger ran faster than he had ever run before.

A monkey sitting in a tree was astonished to see the tiger running so fast. 'Well I never,' he thought, 'it's strange to see a tiger running like that. Something very extraordinary must have happened.' So he called out to him, 'What's happened, brother? Why are you running so fast?'

'Do you think I'm running for fun?' said the tiger, panting. 'I had to flee, or I'd have been snapped up at once.'

'But I've never heard of any animal who could catch or eat you,' said the monkey. 'I don't believe you.'

'If you'd been there, my friend,' said the tiger, 'I'd have seen what you'd have done! It's easy for you to speak from a distance.'

'If I'd been there,' said the monkey, 'I'd have proved to you that there was nothing there at all. You're a fool to be frightened by such nonsense.'

The tiger grew very angry at this. 'Indeed!' he roared, 'I'm a fool am I? And I suppose you're a genius! Come with me — I'll show you the place.'

'I'll gladly come,' said the monkey, 'if you carry me on your back.'

66

'All right, if I must,' said the tiger. 'Get on to my back and let's go.' And with the monkey sitting on him, the tiger made his way back to his hole.

The jackal and his wife had just settled their cubs down when they saw the tiger returning, with the monkey on his back. The jackal's wife quickly rushed over to her cubs to pinch them again; and they started to squeal like the devil.

Then in the same gruff voice as before the jackal said, 'Be quiet! Stop yowling—you'll make yourselves ill.'

'I've told you,' said the jackal's wife, 'they won't stop until you bring them a tiger to eat.'

'I've sent their uncle to go and get a tiger,' said the jackal. 'He'll be bringing it any minute now. Be quiet, children!'

Then he said a little more quietly, 'Aha! Here is your uncle the monkey bringing a tiger. Don't cry any more. Quickly now, give me my jimplong and I'll ballyram him!'

The monkey had been full of bravery up to now. But when he heard the words jimplong and ballyram he didn't dare stay any longer. With a single jump he leapt up into a tree and disappeared.

What can I say to you about the tiger? He fled in such terror that he didn't stop running for two days.

The jackals had no more trouble after that. They lived in their hole with complete peace of mind.

18 The Jackal Inside
the Elephant

THE KING had an elephant which was bigger and better and more beautiful to look at than all his other elephants. He called it his 'state elephant', and used to ride everywhere on it. He loved it dearly.

One day the king's state elephant died. The king was very

distressed; but eventually he said, 'Go and get rid of the body.'

So five hundred men tied thick ropes round the elephant's legs, dragged it into open country and dumped it.

Now there was a jackal living in the area who hadn't eaten properly for many days. When he saw the dead elephant lying there, he fell upon it joyfully and began to eat. He was so famished that he ate his way right into the elephant's stomach, and still went on eating. Two days passed like this, and still the jackal sat inside the elephant's stomach, eating and eating. Meanwhile the elephant's hide had shrivelled in the sun and the entrance to its stomach had narrowed; and of course the jackal had grown fat from eating so much. He was now in serious difficulty. However much he tried, he just couldn't get out of the elephant's stomach. What was to be done?

Three farmers happened to be passing that way. When the jackal saw them, a plan formed in his head. 'Hey, brothers,' he called from inside the elephant's stomach. 'Can you give the king a message? If fifty jars of melted butter can be smeared on my stomach, I shall stand up again.'

'Listen,' said the farmers in great astonishment, 'listen to what the elephant is saying! Come on, let's go and tell the king.' So they quickly made their way to the king and said, 'Your Majesty, that elephant who died has spoken to us: it says that if fifty jars of melted butter are smeared on its stomach it will stand up again. Send the fifty jars quickly!'

The king was indescribably happy when he heard this. 'What are fifty jars of butter if my elephant can be made to live again!' he said. 'Take a thousand jars of butter to smear his stomach with.'

So a thousand porters carried a thousand jars of melted butter and placed them next to the elephant. Two thousand men joined in the task of smearing its stomach with the butter. For seven days nothing but 'Bring the butter, pour the butter' was heard there.

The Jackal Inside the Elephant

At the end of the seven days the jackal could see that the elephant's hide was nice and soft, the entrance to its stomach had greatly widened, and that he could now get out if he wished. 'Brothers,' he called to everybody, 'I'm now about to stand up. Move away a little in case I stagger and fall on you if my head spins.'

Immediately there was complete uproar. Everyone pushed and shoved at those in front of them and shouted, 'Move, get out of the way, you fools! The elephant is getting up — we'll be flattened!'

Nobody stayed. They took to their heels, leaving the jars and everything behind them, without once looking back to see whether the elephant had stood up or was still lying down. 'It's time for me to get away now,' thought the jackal; and he quickly scrambled out of the elephant's stomach and ran off.

19 Majantali Sarkar

IN A VILLAGE there were two cats. One of them lived in the milkmen's house and got milk, cream, butter and curds to eat. The other lived in the fishermen's house and got nothing but beatings and kicks. The milkmen's cat was very fat, and walked along with his chest puffed out. The fishermen's cat was all skin and bone: he tottered as he walked, and

wondered how he might become fat like the milkmen's cat.

Eventually he said to the milkmen's cat one day, 'Brother, why don't you come to my house today and have something to eat?'

This was a dishonest invitation: he didn't get enough to eat himself, so what could he offer a visitor? 'If the milkmen's cat comes round to my house,' he thought, 'he'll get beaten like me and die. Then I shall go and live with the milkmen.'

This is exactly what happened. As soon as the milkmen's cat came to the fishermen's house, the fishermen said, 'Aha! That thieving, milk-and-curds eating, milkmen's cat has come to eat up our fish. Thrash him!'

And they gave him such a beating that the poor thing died. The skinny cat knew that this would happen, and had already appeared at the milkmen's house. He ate such a quantity of cream and curds that he was fat in no time. He stopped speaking to other cats from now on, and called himself 'Majantali Sarkar'.

One day Majantali Sarkar took pen and paper and set off on a walk. He found his way into the forest, where he saw three tiger-cubs playing. 'Come on now, give me your rent!' he said, collaring them — and the cubs were terrified by his pen and paper and his stern manner. They rushed to their mother and cried, 'Come quickly, mother — come and see who it is and what he wants!'

The tigress came and said to Majantali, 'Who are you, my dear? Where have you come from? What do you want?'

'I am a servant of the king,' said Majantali. 'My name is Majantali. Where's your rent? You are living on land owned by the king.'

'I've never heard anything about rent before,' said the tigress. 'We're just forest-dwellers, and anyone who comes our way gets caught and eaten. But sit down a little — the tiger will be back soon.'

Majantali sat down under a tall tree and began to look around cautiously. In a little while he saw the tiger approaching, and he quickly climbed right to the top of the tree, leaving his pen and paper on the ground.

The tigress told the tiger everything that had happened, and I can't tell you how angry he was! 'Where is the villain?' he roared, snarling terribly. 'I'll break his neck!'

'What is it, tiger — aren't you going to pay your rent?' said Majantali from the top of the tree. 'Come on up.'

Baring his teeth and scowling, the tiger roared again and leapt up into the tree in two jumps. But it wasn't easy to catch Majantali: he was a small, light animal and could perch on branches too thin to bear the weight of such a heavy tiger. Mad with fury, the huge beast jumped again — and slipped. As he fell his head got caught between two branches; his neck broke, and he died.

Majantali hurried down to the tiger and scratched him across the nose three or four times. Then he called to the tigress, 'Come and look — see what I've done! See what comes of being rude to me!'

The tigress almost fainted from fright when he showed her. 'Majantali, sir, I beg you,' she said with folded paws, 'don't kill us as well. We'll be your servants from now on.'

'Very well,' said Majantali, 'serve me faithfully and feed me well, and you shall live.'

After this Majantali lived with the tigress and her cubs. He ate plentifully and rode around on the backs of the cubs. The poor beasts lived in fear of their lives, and thought him the most powerful person in the world.

One day the tigress came to him and said imploringly, 'Majantali, sir, there are only tiny animals in this forest — too small to fill your stomach. There's a bigger forest over the river, where much larger animals live. Let's go there.'

'All right,' said Majantali, 'let's go there.' The tigress and her cubs crossed the river in no time. But where was Majantali? The tigress and her cubs looked hard — and saw that Majantali Sarkar was fighting for his life in the middle of the river! The current was sweeping him along, and he was near to drowning from the force of the waves.

Majantali was well aware that another couple of waves would be the end of him. But he was rescued just in time: one of the tiger-cubs dragged him out on to the bank. He would certainly have drowned otherwise.

But Majantali Sarkar didn't let the tigers know this. As soon as he was up on the bank his eyes turned bright red with anger and he started to slap the cub who had rescued him, and cursed him over and over again. Then he said, 'You wretched idiot, now see what you've done! I was doing some complex calculations when you pulled me out — and now I've lost track of them all. I'd just worked out the number of waves in the river, the number of fish and the amount of water. You fool, you messed up everything by barging in like that! When I go to the king without the calculations he wanted, it won't be funny for you.'

The tigress came running when she heard this and said with folded paws, 'Majantali, sir, he made a mistake, please pardon him this time. He's ignorant — he hasn't had any schooling, so he didn't know what he was doing.'

'Very well,' said Majantali, 'I'll forgive him this time. But be careful! Don't let this happen again.' And he went off to dry his wet coat in the sun.

It wasn't easy to find a place where the sun shone through the thick forest. The only thing to do was climb to the top of a tall tree; and when Majantali did so he saw that there was a large buffalo lying dead in a clearing. He quickly went to the body and gave it a few bites and scratches; then he returned to the tigers and said, 'I've just killed a buffalo. Bring it at once.'

The tigress and her cubs hurried along and found that there was indeed a buffalo lying there. The four of them only just managed to drag it back. 'How strong Majantali must be,' they thought as they struggled with it.

On another day they said to Majantali, 'Majantali, sir, there are big elephants and rhinoceroses in this forest. Let's go and kill them sometime.'

'Why not?' said Majantali. 'Elephants and rhinoceroses will suit me fine. Let's go today.'

So he and the tigers went off to hunt elephant and rhinoceros. On the way the tigress asked him, 'Majantali, sir, will you do the killing or the beating?' She wanted to know whether he would lie in wait to kill the animals, or round them up by beating and driving them through the forest.

'No animal is going to be frightened by my beating,' thought Majantali; and he answered, 'You think you could kill all the animals that I'd beat forward? No—you do the beating and I'll do the killing.'

'That's right,' said the tigress, 'how could we ever kill all those enormous animals? Come on, children, we'll do the beating.'

And the tigress and her cubs made their way to the other side of the forest, and roaring tremendously started to drive the animals forward. Majantali sat under a tree, and began to tremble with fear when he heard the animals' cries.

In a little while a porcupine came hurrying towards him, rattling its quills, and with a shriek Majantali went and hid under a root of the tree; but at the same time an elephant passed by, and it trod on the root with the side of one of its feet. Poor Majantali's ribs were broken under the weight, and he was done for.

'Majantali must have killed lots of animals by now,' thought the tigers after beating for a long time. 'Let's go and see.' But when they came and saw the state he was in they wailed, 'Oh Majantali, sir, what has happened?'

'What do you expect?' said Majantali. 'You sent me such tiny animals! I laughed so much when I saw them that my chest burst.'

And with that, Majantali Sarkar died.

20 *The Ant and the Elephant and the Brahmin's Servant*

THERE WAS ONCE an ant, and he and his wife were very fond of one another.

One day his wife said, 'Listen, husband, if I die before you, you must throw me into the Holy Ganges. You will do that, won't you?'

'Yes, dear wife, of course I shall,' said the ant. 'And if I die before you, you must throw me into the Holy Ganges. You will do that, won't you?'

'Of course I shall — you know that,' said the ant's wife.

This is how they talked, until one day the ant's wife did die. The ant wept sorely, and then remembered, 'Now I must take her and throw her into the Holy Ganges.'

So he lifted his wife on to his shoulders and went off towards the Ganges. The Ganges was a long way away and it would take him a long time to get there. He carried his wife for a whole day, and when evening came he saw that he had reached the king's elephant-pen — where all the royal elephants were kept. The ant had had a very hard day, so he took his wife into the pen and sat down for a rest. There was an enormous elephant tethered nearby — the king's state elephant. The elephant was swinging his trunk and snorting through it, and the ant and his wife were blown up into the air by the blasts. 'Watch out,' called the ant, but the elephant couldn't hear him. He snorted again, and again the ants were blown into the air. So the ant grew very angry and shouted, 'Watch out! Mind what you're doing, or you'll be sorry, you good-for-nothing brute!'

'Well I never,' thought the elephant, 'I wonder who's insulting me from down there in such a little voice. I can't see anyone.' And he began to scrape the ground with his foot.

The ant was now in great danger. 'Dear me—I shall be squashed flat,' he thought. But a moment later he found that he had escaped, for he had slipped into one of the little holes on the underside of the elephant's foot, and his wife was safe too.

Who could describe how happy he now was! He sat inside the hole and started to burrow into the elephant's flesh. He didn't stop burrowing until he and his wife had reached right into the elephant's brain.

The elephant was made very ill by this. He did nothing but shake his head, trumpet and charge madly to and fro. 'Alas, alas,' said everyone when they saw him, 'what has happened to him?' No one knew that an ant had got into the elephant's brain. If they had known, and if they'd smeared the bottom of the elephant's foot with sugar, then the sweet smell would have lured out the ant at once. But they didn't know. Doctors were called, and the elephant was soon dead from the medicine they prescribed.

That night the elephant came to the king in a dream and said, 'Your Majesty, I have worked very hard for you — please take me to the Holy Ganges.'

In the morning when he was up the king gave the order, 'Take my elephant and throw him into the Ganges.'

At once two or three hundred people tied thick ropes round the elephant's legs and with a 'Heave-ho! Heave-ho!' dragged him towards the Ganges. He was an immensely big elephant, and it was very hard to move him. The men would pull him a little way, then drop the ropes and sit down panting.

A Brahmin happened to be walking past at the time, and there was a servant with him. When the servant saw the king's men sitting and panting, he said, 'An elephant as big as a mouse — and three hundred men out of breath at pulling him! I could carry him on my own.'

The three hundred men jumped up when they heard this. 'A likely story,' they said. 'If three hundred of us can't manage it, how can you do so on your own? All right then — we shan't drag the elephant any further until you've been put to trial. Come on, let's go to the king and see how strong this fellow is!'

So they left the elephant in the fields and went back together to the king. 'We ask you, Your Majesty, to try this man,' they said. 'Three hundred of us were panting and struggling to move your elephant, and he says that he could do it on his own. We shan't touch your elephant again until you have passed judgement.'

The king turned to the Brahmin's servant and asked, 'Is this true? Can you really carry the elephant on your own?'

The servant bowed humbly before the king and said, 'I can

indeed, if Your Majesty orders me to do so. But first I must have a bite to eat.'

'Give him two pounds of rice, with lentils and vegetables,' said the king. 'Eat your fill first, then lift the elephant.'

The servant laughed at this and said, 'Your Majesty, two pounds of rice is chicken-feed — you think I can move an elephant on that?'

'What do you want then?' asked the king.

'Not very much, Your Majesty,' said the servant. 'A ton of rice, two goats and a ton of curds should be enough.'

'Very well, you shall have it,' said the king, 'but you must eat it all.'

'I shall, Your Majesty,' said the servant.

The Brahmin's servant ate the ton of rice, the two goats and the ton of curds, and had a good nap. Then he wrapped up the elephant in his napkin and tied him into a tight bundle. He attached the bundle to the end of a stick and lifted the stick, with the bundle hanging from it, on to his shoulders. And singing merrily and chewing at least forty betel-leaves at once, he set off towards the Ganges. The king was open-mouthed with astonishment, and the three hundred men too; and everyone rushed off home to tell the news.

Meanwhile the servant had walked a long way, and the sun was glaring down on him. He went on walking a long way further, but eventually he said to himself, 'Phew! What dreadful heat! My throat's terribly parched — a little water should help.'

And just then he noticed a small pond a little way off, with a thatched hut beside it. The servant laid his bundle down by the pond, went up to the hut and found a little girl sitting there.

'Young friend,' he said to her, 'I'm very thirsty — could you give me a little water?'

'We've only a jar of water left,' said the girl. 'If I give you some, what will my father drink when he comes in from the fields?'

'Well well,' said the servant angrily, 'so you can't spare a drop of water. All right — let's see where you get your water from after this!'

And he went down to the pond and started to drink the water in great gulps. For as long as there was water in the pond, his gulps were all that could be heard. Soon he had drunk up all the water in the pond, and as he drank his stomach swelled — first like a drum, then like an elephant, finally like an absolute mountain. But the Brahmin's servant now found that he couldn't keep an entire pondful of water down in his stomach. There was only one thing to do — he quickly swallowed a banyan tree as well. The banyan tree stuck in his throat like a stopper, and the water was held in.

The Brahmin's servant was now very happy, and he lay down beside the pond for a rest. His stomach towered higher than a palm tree — it was like a mountain! The little girl's father was working in the fields at the time: 'Good heavens! What on earth is that?' he wondered when he saw the mountainous stomach, and at once he hurried back home.

When he got there his daughter said, 'Father, father, see what this wicked man has done! He asked me for water. There was only a jar of water left — if I'd given it to him, what would you have had when you came home? And because I wouldn't give him any, he drank up all the water in our pond!'

The two of them had got nearer to the servant as they talked and suddenly the little girl crinkled up her nose and said, 'Ugh! What a stink! Look at that, father — he must have brought a rotting mouse tied up in his bundle.'

And pressing a corner of her dress against her nose with one hand, she picked up the bundle with two fingers of the other and threw it, elephant and all. She threw it so far that it landed in the Ganges itself.

What do you think her father did now? He tightened his belt, clenched his teeth, and gave the Brahmin's servant's stomach a kick. It wasn't an ordinary kick! The force of it knocked out the banyan tree, and all the water in the servant's stomach came gushing out after it, so that the little girl, the hut and their possessions were swept right away. Only the little girl's father and the Brahmin's servant were left behind, and the two of them embraced each other warmly.

When they had finished embracing each other the little girl's father said, 'Well, my friend, I've never met anyone as mighty as you. Fancy drinking up a whole pondful of water!'

'But I've never met anyone as strong as you, my friend,' said the Brahmin's servant. 'Fancy emptying my stomach with a single kick!'

They started to argue hotly about this, each of them saying the other was stronger. Who could say now which one was right?

After arguing for a long time they decided that they would go to a large market and have a wrestling-match there, so that it could be seen which one was the stronger.

So the two of them set off towards the market, and on the way they met a fisherwoman. The fisherwoman had a basket of fish on her head and was going to the market to sell them. 'And where are you going?' she asked when she saw the two men.

'We're going to the market to have a wrestling-match,' they said.

'The market's a long way off, my dears,' she said. 'Why go to the trouble of walking all the way there? Wrestle inside my basket instead. I'll be able to tell which of you is winning from the tipping of my basket as you wrestle.'

'What a good idea,' they said. 'We can have our wrestling-match without a walk.'

So they got into the fisherwoman's basket and started to wrestle, and the fisherwoman continued on her way to the market with the basket on her head.

But then a strange thing happened. There was a vicious, destructive hawk in the district who would swallow any cows, buffaloes, elephants or horses that he could find. The fisherwoman was the only person who was a match for him, and whenever he tried to take her basket she gave him such a scolding that he flew off in a panic. But this made him all the angrier and he was determined that one day he would snatch away the basket somehow.

That day the hawk was out looking for food, and the whirring of his wings could be heard from a long way away.

A cowherd had brought his seven hundred buffaloes out into the fields to graze. 'Good grief,' he thought to himself when he heard the noise of the hawk's wings, 'there's that hawk — he'll eat up all my buffaloes! What shall I do?'

The cowherd stuffed the seven hundred buffaloes into a corner of his loin-cloth and ran back home like the wind.

'What's happened?' asked his family. 'Why have you been running so fast?'

'What else could I do?' he said. 'The hawk was coming to eat my buffaloes.'

'But where have you left them?' they asked.

'Do you think I'd leave them behind?' he said. 'I've brought them with me.'

'But where are they?' they asked.

'Here they are,' he said. And he opened up his loin-cloth and seven hundred buffaloes rolled out.

His family were overjoyed when they saw them and said, 'What a good thing you put them there — the hawk would have eaten them all today if you hadn't.'

The hawk meanwhile was still flying about in search of food, and in the fisherwoman's basket two burly men were still wrestling. The fisherwoman was thinking about them all the time, and had forgotten about the hawk. And just at that moment the hawk caught sight of her, swooped, and seized the basket off her head.

The king's daughter had just sat down on the roof of the palace, and a maid was combing her hair.

'Come and look, maid,' she said, closing her eyes, 'something's fallen into my eye.'

The maid twisted a corner of her sari, licked it, and dabbing at the princess's eye extracted a tiny, delicate black object.

'What a lovely little thing!' said the princess. 'What is it?'

The maid couldn't say what it was. Everyone in the palace came to look at it, but no one could say what it was. The king came, his ministers came, but they didn't know what it was either.'

Then the king called some great scholars to examine it.

They had all sorts of machines with them, through which an ant could seem as big as an elephant. They peered through the machines and said, 'What we see is a basket: there are some fish inside it, and two men having a wrestling-match.'

TRANSLATOR'S NOTE

The Stupid Tiger and Other Tales is not my own collection of Bengali folk-tales; neither have I told the stories in my own words. It is a translation of one of the classic children's books of Bengal — **Tuntunir Bai** ("The Tailor-bird's Book"), by Upendrakishore Raychaudhuri (1863-1915). I have changed the title, and reduced the number of stories from twenty-six to twenty; but otherwise I have tried to be true to the letter and spirit of the original.

Though rural in its contents, the book is a product of Calcutta — capital of India until 1911, and by then established as a great cultural and educational centre. Upendrakishore was the doyen of one of Calcutta's most versatile and enterprising families. He was an artist and musician as well as a writer; he was a pioneer in book illustration techniques, founding his own printing company; and his children's magazine **Sandeś** (which still flourishes) had wide social influence. His son Sukumar Ray was a brilliant children's writer, and his grandson Satyajit Ray, the internationally acclaimed film director, has written books that maintain the family tradition.

Tuntunir Bai was first published in 1910, with the author's own illustrations. It met a growing need for good children's fiction; but it also perhaps sprang from a movement to preserve Bengal's rich folklore. In 1907 Dakshinaranjan Mitra Majumdar had published his **Thákurmár Jhuli** ("Grandmother's Bag"), a classic collection of fairy tales; and by 1917 sufficient material had been collected for Dinesh Chandra Sen, the great historian of Bengali language and literature, to give a course of lectures on the Folk Literature of Bengal to Calcutta University.

There are two reasons why **Tuntunir Bai** has remained very popular with Bengali children. Firstly, Upendrakishore rightly judged that this particular strain in the folk literature, the humorous animal story, was most likely to appeal to urban children, from whom the complex religious and mythological traditions behind Bengal's many supernatural tales were increasingly remote. Secondly, he was a stylist of genius, writing a simple, lucid Bengali that children could read themselves. Dakshinaranjan tried to preserve the mannerisms and archaisms of the countrywoman who told him the stories, and his collections have dated; Upendrakishore used his own words, and no doubt added touches of his own invention. I hope that for English readers too, young or old, his witty, natural, unpatronizing voice will be one of the main charms of these tales.

William Radice